Get Moving

Lisa Greatho

Consultant

Gina Montefusco, RN
Children's Hospital Los Angeles
Los Angeles, California

Publishing Credits

Dona Herweck Rice, *Editor-in-Chief*
Lee Aucoin, *Creative Director*
Don Tran, *Print Production Manager*
Timothy J. Bradley, *Illustration Manager*
Chris McIntyre, M.A.Ed., *Editorial Director*
James Anderson, M.S.Ed., *Editor*
Stephanie Reid, *Photo Editor*
Rachelle Cracchiolo, M.S.Ed., *Publisher*

Image Credits

Teacher Created Materials

5301 Oceanus Drive
Huntington Beach, CA 92649-1030
http://www.tcmpub.com
ISBN 978-1-4333-3089-6

Table of Contents

Be the Best You Can Be!

You make many choices each day. You choose what to wear and how to style your hair. You choose your friends and whom to sit with on the bus. You pick what sports to play and which books to read. You might help choose where your family goes on vacation. Those are lots of decisions!

There are plenty of smaller choices you make each day, too. You choose what to eat for lunch and what snack to have after school. You might choose what to do after your homework—whether to play outside, play video games, go on the computer, or watch TV. Those decisions might not seem important. Yet they have a big impact on your life.

Think About It

We would not be able to make decisions like these without our brains. The **cerebrum** (suh-REE-bruhm) is the biggest part of your brain. You use it to figure out math problems and draw pictures. But it also controls the muscles that you want to move. So you cannot run, dance, or throw a ball without it!

cerebrum

cerebellum

brain stem

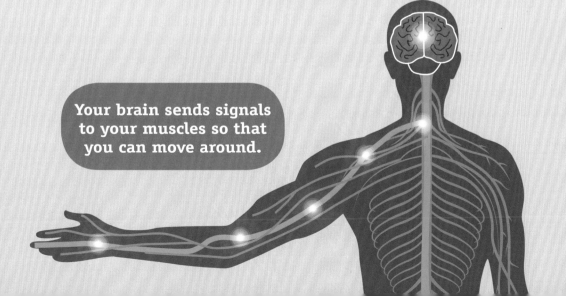

Your brain sends signals to your muscles so that you can move around.

Getting Fit

There is a lot of talk about kids needing to "get fit." First Lady Michelle Obama has made it her goal to help kids lead healthy lives. But what does it mean to be fit? There are two keys to having a fit body—eating right and being active.

When it comes to eating right, a good place to start is by eating more fruits, vegetables, and whole grains. Eat a variety of these foods each day.

Do not eat junk food. It is filled with sugar, fat, and salt. That does not mean you have to give up your favorite foods for good. It does mean that you need to take charge of your health. Start a food journal and write down the foods you eat for a week. Read the **nutrition** (noo-TRISH-uhn) labels. Then, eat a fruit or a vegetable instead of a food you should not be eating often, such as potato chips or candy.

MyPlate

The **MyPlate** guide shows us the types of food we should eat at each meal. It also shows us the proportion that each type of food should represent on our plates.

Mrs. Obama shows children that being active can be fun!

Smart Substitute

When you are eating fast food, have some apple or pear slices on the side instead of french fries. For breakfast, try yogurt and a banana instead of a sugary doughnut. Your body will thank you!

Get Off the Couch!

The average kid spends about four hours a day sitting in front of the TV or computer, or playing video games. That is a long time to be inactive. Take a sports break every hour or so. Play outside and get some exercise.

Be Active

The other piece of the fitness puzzle is being active. Think about how many hours a day you sit. You spend most of your day at school sitting at a desk. Then, when you get home, how much time do you spend in front of the TV or computer? Do not forget the time you spend doing homework, reading books, and eating. Now add up all those hours you spend sitting. You might be shocked!

The good news is that it takes just one hour of activity per day to get and stay fit. You do not need to be active for 60 minutes all at once. It can include time walking to school and running around at recess. It can be the time you spend riding your bike, dancing, or skateboarding. If you play sports, that counts, too!

What is the big deal about being fit? Well, you may already know that you feel better when you eat healthy foods and get regular exercise. You are not as tired during the day, and you sleep better at night. You can climb stairs without huffing and puffing. You can run faster and jump higher. That might seem like enough—but there is much more!

Being fit actually adds years to your life. It keeps your heart healthy. It makes your bones and muscles strong. It cuts your risk of getting diseases like **diabetes** (dahy-uh-BEE-teez). It keeps your **blood pressure** and **cholesterol** (kuh-LES-tuh-rohl) levels low.

Being fit does more than make you look and feel better. It makes sense to stay healthy!

PRESSURE

Blood Pressure

Your heart pumps blood through your blood vessels. As the blood moves, it pushes against the walls of your blood vessels with force. You can measure this force by taking your blood pressure.

Staying fit allows your body to give you the strength and energy to go for the gold!

Did You Know?

The foods we eat have **calories**, which give us energy. But many of us get way too many calories from foods that have no nutrients, like soda and candy. These are called *empty calories*. Maximize your energy by eating fruits, vegetables, and grains.

Nutrition Facts

Serving Size 1/6 package (60g)
Servings Per Container 6

Amount Per Serving		Mix Prepared
Calories	260	360
Calories from Fat	80	150

		% Daily Value*	
Total Fat 9g*		**14%**	**26%**
Saturated Fat 3.5g		**18%**	**30%**
Cholesterol 0mg		**0%**	**1%**
Sodium 360mg		**15%**	**20%**
Total Carbohydrate 46g		**15%**	**16%**
Dietary Fiber 1g		**4%**	**4%**
Sugars 28g			
Protein 2g			
Vitamin A		0%	10%
Vitamin C		0%	0%
Calcium		15%	25%
Iron		6%	6%

*Amount in mix

Values are based on a 2,000

Getting Started

Now you know how important it is to be fit. But you might be thinking: *How do I get started?* Well, the first step is to shut off the TV and turn off the computer. The less time you spend sitting, the better. The good news is, being active is fun!

Some kids like to play organized sports like soccer, baseball, and basketball. Others love gymnastics and dance. The best activities for you are the ones that you love to do. It does not matter if you have a bunch of friends to join you or if you are by yourself. Just get moving!

Awesome Activities

- Hop on your bike and go for a ride.
- Grab a soccer ball and practice your moves.
- Strap on your rollerblades and take a spin.
- Pick up a basketball and see how many baskets you can sink.
- See how many times you can spin a plastic hoop around your waist.

A Happier You!

Do you ever wonder why you feel so good after you go outside to play? When you are active for more than 20 minutes, your body releases chemicals called **endorphins** (en-DAWR-fins). Endorphins put you in a better mood and make you feel happier!

Burning Calories

Whatever your favorite activity may be, all exercise is good for you. Anytime you are active, you are working muscles and burning calories. Here are the number of calories you burn doing about one hour of the following activities. Which one is your favorite?

Activity	Calories Burned (per hour)*
Dancing	230
Playing basketball	305
Riding a bike	425
Bowling	120
Hiking	305
Running	425
Skating	365
Playing soccer	365
Walking	150
Throwing a plastic disc	120
Playing volleyball	185
Swimming	305
Skateboarding	245
Playing football (touch)	425
Practicing martial arts	550

*Based on a person who weighs about 100 pounds
Source: United States Department of Agriculture

Stuck Inside? No Problem!

Do you live in a place that gets lots of rain or snow? Or do you live in an area that is too hot or too cold to play outside? Here are some ideas for staying fit when you are stuck indoors:

- Play hide-and-seek with a friend or a sibling and find all the great hiding spots in your house.

- Put on a dance-workout DVD. Or, just turn on some music and come up with your own moves.

- Play a video game on a system that gets you moving.

- Set up an obstacle course using things in your house. Crawl under tables, do flips on the couch, and run up and down the stairs (with your parents' permission, of course).

- See how many sit-ups or push-ups you can do in three minutes. Rest for a minute and then try to break your record!

- Jump rope in an open area of your home. Use a stopwatch to count how long you can go without stopping.

Start Small

Small changes in your day can lead to a big change in how you feel. There are many things you can do.

First, turn off the TV when you are eating meals. This is a great time to talk about your day with your family. When you do watch TV, do not snack. Get up and move during commercials. Dance or do sit-ups. Do anything that gets your heart pumping.

When you are out, ask your parents to park far away from where you are going. The extra walk will be good for them, too. When you have a choice of taking an elevator, an escalator, or the stairs, pick the stairs!

Ask your parents if you can replace the chair at your family's computer with an exercise ball for at least part of the day. You will have fun on the computer while also building your **core muscles**!

Try to work even just one of these changes into your day. Soon, you will not have to think about it. Try to get your whole family to join you!

Did You Know?

When you exercise and breathe more deeply, your brain gets more **oxygen** (OK-si-juhn). This extra oxygen can give your brain a boost and can help you do well on schoolwork and tests.

Get Moving!

The *Let's Move!* program started by First Lady Michelle Obama has more great ideas for being active. Check it out at **www.letsmove.gov**.

Warm up!

Have you ever been injured playing a sport? Maybe you **sprained** your ankle. Or you might have strained a muscle. Ouch! Some sprains can hurt for weeks or even months! This can happen if your muscles are not warmed up.

For about five to ten minutes before any activity, try walking in place. Or, do a gentle version of the activity you are about to do. For instance, if you are going to be playing baseball, start by tossing the ball to a teammate. If you are going to go for a run, try a light jog at first.

Warming up really does make your muscles warmer before you put them to work. It gets your heart pumping. And that brings more oxygen to your muscles.

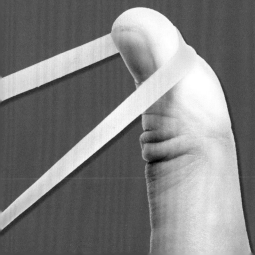

Cold Snap!

A cold muscle is like a rubber band that has been in the freezer. Stretch it too far, and it may just snap! That is what often leads to painful muscle tears and strains that need be treated by a doctor. So, warm up first to avoid injury, and that muscle (just like the rubber band) will stretch just fine.

Stretching Tips

Stretching feels good. And it is especially important to do before you exercise. Here are some things to keep in mind as you stretch:

- Stretching should not hurt. If it does, relax and find a point that feels comfortable.
- Take deep breaths as you stretch.
- Stretch slowly (do not bounce).
- Hold your stretches for about 30 seconds.

The Benefits of Being Fit

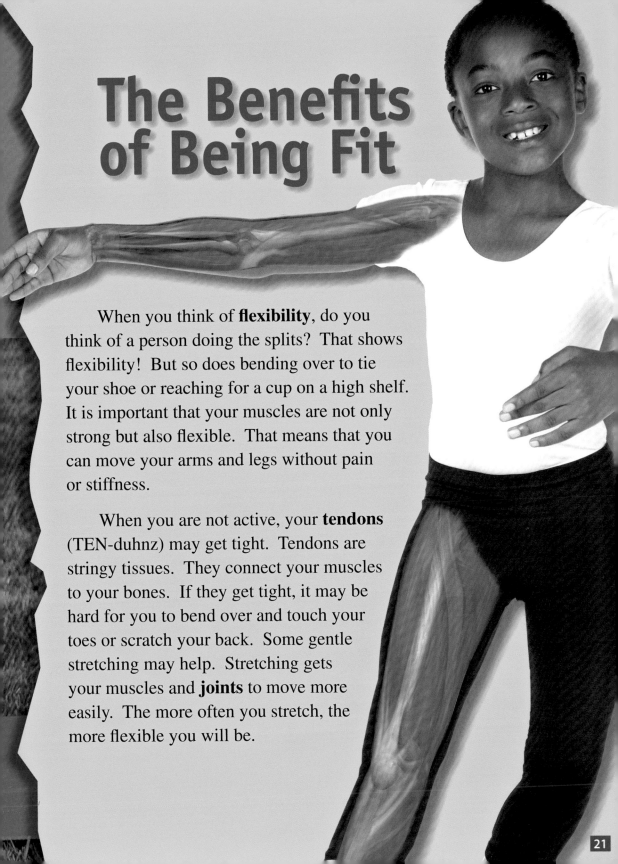

When you think of **flexibility**, do you think of a person doing the splits? That shows flexibility! But so does bending over to tie your shoe or reaching for a cup on a high shelf. It is important that your muscles are not only strong but also flexible. That means that you can move your arms and legs without pain or stiffness.

When you are not active, your **tendons** (TEN-duhnz) may get tight. Tendons are stringy tissues. They connect your muscles to your bones. If they get tight, it may be hard for you to bend over and touch your toes or scratch your back. Some gentle stretching may help. Stretching gets your muscles and **joints** to move more easily. The more often you stretch, the more flexible you will be.

Move Your Body

Have you ever looked at a superhero and wished you could have muscles just like him or her? One benefit to getting fit is building your muscles. You might think you need to lift weights to build muscles. But lifting weights is not good for you while you are still growing.

Anaerobic (an-uh-ROH-bik) **exercises** will build your muscles. These kinds of activities use your own body weight. They increase your strength and power. They require a big burst of energy. To do these exercises, your body must use energy stored in your muscles. Push-ups, jumping rope, and sprinting are all anaerobic exercises.

Major Muscle Groups

Here are some of your body's major muscle groups.

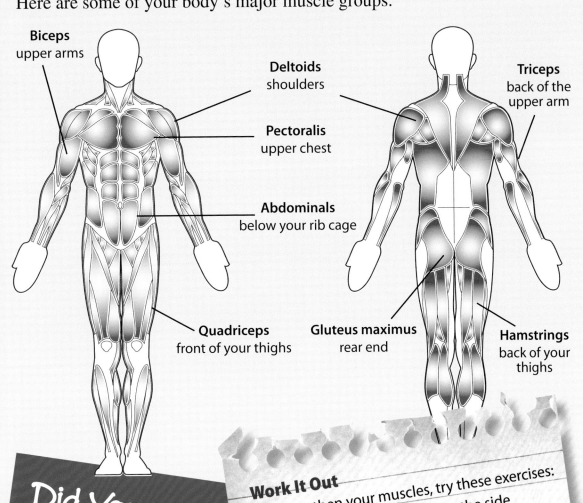

Biceps
upper arms

Deltoids
shoulders

Pectoralis
upper chest

Abdominals
below your rib cage

Triceps
back of the
upper arm

Quadriceps
front of your thighs

Gluteus maximus
rear end

Hamstrings
back of your
thighs

Did You Know?

The human body has over 600 muscles! Each one is made out of thousands of small fibers.

Work It Out
To strengthen your muscles, try these exercises:
Deltoids: hold your arms out to the side
Pectoralis: do push-ups or chest presses
Abdominals: do sit-ups or squat exercises
Biceps: swing a bat, throw a ball, jump rope
Triceps: swim, play basketball
Quadriceps: stand up, run, bike
Hamstrings: touch your toes, walk backwards
Gluteus maximus: climb stairs, hike

Did You Know?

Your heart beats about 100,000 times a day!

Do you ever feel like you cannot catch your breath when you jog, dance, or walk up stairs? These are **aerobic** (ai-ROH-bik) **exercises**. Aerobic means "needing air." These exercises last longer than anaerobic exercises. They use up more energy. You need to take in a lot of oxygen to do them. This makes your heart and lungs work nonstop. You can feel your heart beating faster. You breathe harder, too.

Aerobic exercise is a test of your **endurance** (en-DOOR-uhns). That is a measure of how long your body can stay active without quitting. When you do aerobic activities, your heart and lungs grow stronger. The stronger they are, the longer you can run, dance, bike, or swim.

Feel the Pulse

When your heart beats, it pumps your blood. The heart pushes your blood through your body. This makes your pulse. Your pulse tells you how fast your heart is beating. You can feel your pulse by placing your fingers over your wrist. You can also feel your pulse on your neck.

Set Your Goal!

No matter what you do in life, it helps to have goals. You might want to improve your math grades or keep your room cleaner. Or a goal could be to become a better speller or a faster swimmer. But it is not enough to have a goal. You need to create a step-by-step plan to get there. It takes more than a desire to reach your goal. It takes hard work!

When your goal is to become more fit, it is best to take small steps. A good first step might be cutting out soda and other sugary drinks. Instead, drink water every day. That is eight cups of water. Or you can challenge yourself to be active for at least 20 minutes per day—and then work your way up to 60 minutes. Remember, it does not have to be all at once.

So, set your goal and make a plan. You will be surprised how small steps can lead to big changes!

Think About Your Drink

Our bodies need water to work properly, and most of us do not drink enough. By the time you feel thirsty, you may already be suffering from **dehydration** (dee-high-DRAY-shuhn). When you are active, your body loses water—that is *you* sweating! So drink plenty of water every day—and drink extra when you are active!

Lab: Check Your Pulse

Checking your pulse is important when you exercise. It can tell you if you are working your heart too hard or not enough.

Materials

- stopwatch or watch that counts seconds
- sheet of paper
- plastic hoops
- miniature beanbags
- 12 miniature plastic cones

Check Your Pulse

1. Place your index and middle finger on the side of your neck. Move your fingers around until you can feel your blood pulsing. It should feel like a steady beat.

2. Use a stopwatch or a watch with a second hand to take your pulse. Count how many beats you feel in 10 seconds.

3. Multiply the number of beats by 6. That will tell you your heart rate, or pulse, for each minute. A normal heart rate when you are resting is 60 to 100 beats per minute. When you exercise, your target heart rate should be around 175 beats per minute.

Exercise Can Be Fun

4. Check your pulse before exercising. It should be within the normal range. Record your pulse on a sheet of paper.

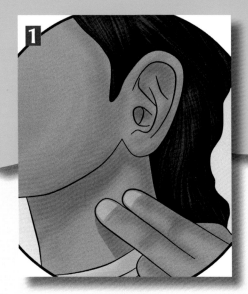

5. Pair up with a partner and toss a beanbag back and forth while one of you spins a plastic hoop. Keep going until someone drops the beanbag or the hoop. If your team lasts the longest, you win!

6. Check and record your pulse. Is your pulse close to the exercise target range? Is your heart working too hard or not enough?

7. Create two identical obstacle courses using plastic cones. Form teams and have each team member race through the course and back. The fastest team wins! Race again and have players hop through the course or walk backwards.

8. Check and record your pulse again. Has your heart rate changed?

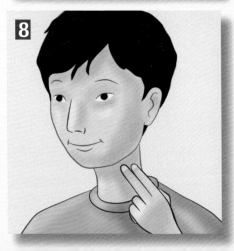

9. Rest for a few minutes and check your pulse again. Is your heart rate returning to normal?

Glossary

aerobic exercises—physical activities that need continuous and large amounts of oxygen to generate energy, such as jogging or walking upstairs

anaerobic exercises—brief, intense physical activities, like weight lifting and sprinting

blood pressure—pressure of the blood on the walls of blood vessels and especially arteries

calorie—a unit of energy that tells you how much energy you can receive from a food or drink

cerebrum—a part of the brain that controls muscle movement and mental functions like thought, reason, emotion, and memory

cholesterol—a waxy substance in your body needed to protect nerves and produce hormones, vitamins, and bile

core muscles—muscles found in the body (minus the legs and arms), including abdominal and back muscles

dehydration—the state in which the body has lost too much water to function properly

diabetes—a disease that affects how the body uses sugar

endorphins—hormones that reduce the sensation of pain and affect emotions

endurance—the ability to withstand hardship, adversity, or stress

flexibility— ability to be bent easily

joint—the point of contact between two bones in the body that allows movement

MyPlate—a graphic organizer that shows the types of foods we should eat at each meal in the proper proportions

nutrition—the science of how living things take in and use food

oxygen—a colorless, tasteless, odorless gas that is necessary for life

sprain—a sudden or severe twisting of a joint with stretching or tearing of ligaments

tendons—a band of connective tissue that links a muscle to a bone

Index

The First Lady's Challenge

She became America's First Lady, but Michelle Obama also had a career in law. That was before she met the future president. In 2008, she and President Barack Obama made history. They became the first African American president and First Lady. They have two daughters. Their names are Sasha and Malia.

Mrs. Obama's role as a mom made her want to help America's children get fit. So she launched a program called *Let's Move!* This program is designed to get kids to be active. So, shut off the TV and computer and go out to play. Ride your bike! Go for a walk! Play a game of tag! Roller skate or skateboard! Mrs. Obama knows that kids who are active and eat healthy foods will grow up to be healthy adults.

Personal Challenge

Check out more about the *Let's Move!* program at **www.letsmove.gov**. Another great program is the *Presidential Champions* program. You can choose from a variety of activities. Then track your progress along the way. Your goal is to see how many points you can earn by being active. Work hard enough, and you can earn a gold medal! Take the *President's Challenge* at **www.presidentschallenge.org**.